Prentice-Hall International, Inc., London
Prentice-Hall of Australia, Pty. Ltd., North Sydney
Prentice-Hall of Canada, Ltd., Toronto
Prentice-Hall of India Private Ltd., New Delhi
Prentice-Hall of Japan, Inc., Tokyo
Prentice-Hall of Southeast Asia Pte. Ltd., Singapore
Whitehall Books Limited, Wellington, New Zealand

10 9 8 7 6 5 4 3 2 1

Library of Congress Cataloging in Publication Data
Edwards, Dorothy.
    My naughty little sister and bad Harry's rabbit.
Summary: *When a little girl managed to get her*
picture in the newspaper with her playmate's favorite
toy, jealousy threatens their friendship.
[*1. Jealousy—Fiction.   2. Friendship—Fiction*]
I. Hughes, Shirley. II. Title.   PZ7.E2518My
[*E*]   *80-18501   ISBN 0-13-608935-6*

My Naughty Little Sister and Bad Harry's Rabbit

Dorothy Edwards &
Shirley Hughes

Prentice-Hall, Inc.
Englewood Cliffs, New Jersey

A long time ago, when I was a little girl,
I had a sister who was very much younger
than me. Although my sister was often naughty,
most of the naughty things she did were
so funny that no one was cross with her
for very long and she made a lot of friends.

Here is a story about one of my sister's
adventures. It is called "My Naughty
Little Sister and Bad Harry's Rabbit."

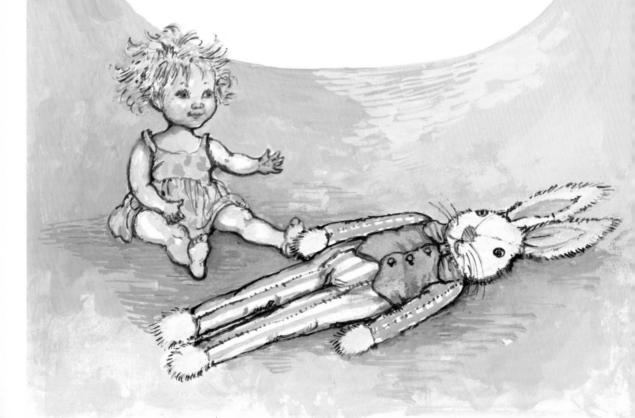

My naughty little sister's friend Bad Harry had a toy
rabbit that was nearly as big as himself, and there was a
time when he took it everywhere he went because
my sister took her poor old doll Rosy-Primrose
everywhere she went.

When my naughty little sister was tired of carrying
Rosy-Primrose, she would sit her down on the ground,
but Harry's rabbit couldn't sit because its legs wouldn't
bend and when Harry leant it against things, it slid
down, so he had to carry it all the time. My naughty
little sister said Bad Harry's rabbit was a nuisance.

"Why don't you leave it at home?" she would say.
But Harry said he would only leave it at home
if my sister left Rosy-Primrose and my sister said
she wouldn't do that. So as they were very stubborn
children, when they went out Rosy-Primrose
and the rabbit had to go too.

Bad Harry had a kind auntie in Canada who used to send him presents and one day his auntie sent him a pair of strong red shoes. It wasn't his birthday or Christmas—she just sent them!

Harry *was* pleased. "Aren't they shiny!" he said. "Like red apples."

"Let's try them on," said Harry's mother. So he kicked off his slippers and stuck out his feet. *But they wouldn't go on.* Those shiny red shoes were much too small for Bad Harry's feet. Bad Harry couldn't believe it. He kicked and banged and shouted, but it was no good.

At last his mother fetched his outdoor shoes and
measured the new ones against them and then
Harry saw they really were too small. So he stopped
being naughty, though he was still cross.

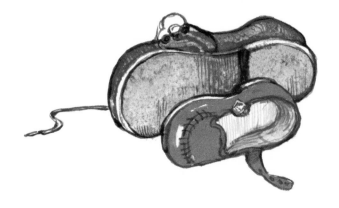

Next day, when our mother and my naughty little sister came to call for Harry and his mother to go shopping, Harry showed them the red shoes. They certainly were very small. They were even too small for my little sister and her feet were littler than Harry's.

While his mother was putting her coat on, Harry fetched his rabbit, and then my little sister had a good idea. She laid Harry's rabbit on the ground and lifted up its right foot and she took the right little red shoe and slipped it on the rabbit's foot and it fit perfectly.

Then she lifted its left foot, and she took the left little red shoe and it fit perfectly too.

Then she stood Harry's rabbit up on the floor and *it didn't fall over*.

"Look, Harry, he's standing now," my sister said, and Harry was so pleased his rabbit could stand on its own, that he wasn't cross any more about the shoes not fitting him.

"I can stand him up when we're shopping or waiting at bus stops now," he said.

And that's just what happened. Whenever our mothers stopped somewhere and my little sister sat Rosy-Primrose on the ground beside her, Bad Harry stood his rabbit beside him. Because it was such a big rabbit, all the people going by stared and stared, and when they saw the red shoes on Harry's rabbit's feet they said, "You are a clever boy," and Harry smiled at them.

Bad Harry liked people saying he was clever, but my naughty little sister didn't. "You're not clever, you Bad Harry," she said. "I'm clever. I put the shoes on, not you."

"He's *my* rabbit," that bad boy said.

Now one of the people going by
was a man with a camera round his
neck, and he lifted it up and took
a picture of Harry and Harry's
rabbit and my little sister and
Rosy-Primrose waiting at a bus stop.

"If I'm lucky I'll get the picture in the paper," the man said, and everyone was very pleased. Harry was so pleased he jumped up and down all the way home and for the next few days he talked and talked about the man taking the photograph and how it would be in the paper if the man was lucky.

And the man *was* lucky and the picture was in the paper and Bad Harry wasn't a bit pleased when his mother showed it to him. There was Harry's toy rabbit standing in the red shoes and Rosy-Primrose sitting on

A little girl with A GOOD IDEA!

the ground and my little sister standing between them smiling and smiling. *But there was no Bad Harry!* Under the picture it said: "A little girl with a good idea."

When his mother read that to him Harry was very angry. "It's not her rabbit, it's my rabbit!" he shouted, and when my sister came round to show them the picture in our paper, in case Harry's mother hadn't seen it, Harry shouted at her. "It's my rabbit, you naughty girl! You are in my rabbit's picture."

My little sister had been sorry that Harry wasn't in the picture too, but when he shouted she stopped being sorry for him. She said, "Well it *was* my good idea."

After that Harry was so cross and nasty that my little sister picked up the newspaper and went straight home with it and told us how cross Harry was.

"Well, I thought Harry would be in the picture," Mother said. "I remember the man kept saying, 'Keep still, Little Boy,' to him. It's a shame, poor child," our mother said. Mother was right too, Harry should have been in that picture.

Because my little sister looked so nice in the newspaper picture, our father went to the photographer's shop, to buy a copy to put in a frame. He brought it home in a big yellow envelope.

Mother was very pleased with it. "What a shame poor Harry wasn't in it too," she said.

Then our father said a funny thing. He said, "Well, it was a rabbit he was taking, not a boy with three heads and six legs!" He took another picture out of the yellow envelope and then he began to laugh and we laughed too.

For there was my naughty little sister and Rosy-Primrose and Bad Harry's rabbit and Bad Harry too, but he had been fidgeting about so much when the picture was taken, that it made him look as if he did have three heads and three pair of legs.

"It was such a good picture the man didn't want to waste it, so he just cut Harry off the end," Father said.

My little sister asked if she could have that picture
to give to Harry and Father said, yes, if she liked,
the photographer had given it to him.

So my little sister took the picture round to Harry
and when Bad Harry saw it he stopped being cross with
her. He looked at himself with the heads and legs and
he was delighted.

"Look at me," he said, "Look at this picture of funny me."

And my sister looked, and Harry's mother looked—and that's just what it was—a picture of funny Harry.

Harry was the *only one you noticed*, for a little boy with
three heads and six legs is much more interesting to
look at than an old doll, or a standing-up rabbit, or
even a naughty little sister.